BY CHRIS BARTON & TOM LICHTENHELD

SHARK v

Well, that depends on if they're . . .

in the ocean . . .

or on railroad tracks.

If they're on
a seesaw . . .

or in hot-air balloons.

or having a
burping contest.

It depends on whether they're bowling . . .

shooting baskets . . .

or going off the high-dive.

EEEEK!!!

Running lemonade stands . . .

trick-or-treating . . .

or giving rides at a carnival.

It can depend on who gets to pick first . . .

who names the game . . .

**and who deals
the cards.**

**But who wins
if they're . . .**

playing hide-and-seek . . .

Performing in a piano recital . . .

or playing *Extreme Zombie-Squirrel Motocross?*

Exploring distant galaxies . . .

or sword fighting
on a tightrope . . .

or . . .

End of the line.

To Erin, for helping me gather steam—and for letting me know when I'm all wet. —C. B.

As always, with love and appreciation to Jan. —T. L.

Little, Brown and Company

Hachette Book Group
237 Park Avenue, New York, NY 10017
Visit our website at www.lb-kids.com

Little, Brown and Company is a division of Hachette Book Group, Inc.
The Little, Brown name and logo are trademarks of Hachette Book Group, Inc.

First Edition: April 2010

Library of Congress Cataloging-in-Publication Data

Barton, Chris.
Shark vs. train / Written by Chris Barton ; Illustrated by Tom Lichtenheld. —1st ed.
p. cm.
Summary: A shark and a train compete in a series of contests on a seesaw,
in hot air balloons, bowling, shooting baskets, playing hide-and-seek, and more.
ISBN 978-0-316-00762-7
[1. Competition (Psychology)—Fiction. 2. Sharks—Fiction. 3. Railroad trains—Fiction.]
I. Lichtenheld, Tom, ill. II. Title. III. Title: Shark versus train.
PZ7.B2849Sh 2010
[E]—dc22
2009017961

10 9 8 7 6 5 4 3

TTP

Printed in China

So, who won?

I lost track.